560C

R0202333563

06/2021

 W9-AYO-570

Angelina Ballerina

Practice
Makes Perfect

Based on the stories by Katharine Holabird
Based on the illustrations by Helen Craig

Ready-to-Read

Simon Spotlight
New York   London   Toronto   Sydney   New Delhi

SIMON SPOTLIGHT

An imprint of Simon & Schuster Children's Publishing Division

1230 Avenue of the Americas, New York, New York 10020

This Simon Spotlight edition May 2021

Illustrations by Mike Deas

For information about special discounts for bulk purchases, please contact Simon & Schuster Special Sales at 1-866-506-1949 or business@simonandschuster.com.

Manufactured in the United States of America 0321 LAK

10 9 8 7 6 5 4 3 2 1

ISBN 978-1-5344-8590-7 (hc)

ISBN 978-1-5344-8589-1 (pbk)

ISBN 978-1-5344-8591-4 (eBook)

It was summertime
in Chipping Cheddar.

All the ballerinas were getting ready for the Summer Festival Dance.

Miss Lilly chose all the partners for the dance.

Angelina could not wait to
find out who her dance
partner would be!

Alice and Flora were
partners.

William and Felicity were
partners.

"Angelina, your partner
is Henry," Miss Lilly said.
"Oh no!" gasped Angelina.

Miss Lilly began to teach
the steps for the Summer
Festival Dance.

Everyone followed
along . . . everyone except
Henry.

He jumped
instead of bowing.

He lifted his right arm
instead of his left.

Angelina tried to help.
"Just follow me,"
she said. "I will show
you the steps."

Then Henry twirled too
fast and bumped into
Angelina.
"Ouch!" she cried.

After class,
Angelina asked Miss Lilly
for a new partner.

"Henry cannot get anything right," Angelina complained.

"No one is perfect
on their first try,"
Miss Lilly said.

"Keep practicing together.
You will become
wonderful partners."

The next day,
Henry still mixed up
his left and right.

He still bumped
into Angelina.

"I will never be
a good dancer,"
Henry sniffled.

Angelina remembered
what Miss Lilly had said.

"We just need to
keep practicing,"
Angelina said.
"Practice makes perfect!"

Angelina practiced with
Henry every day.

"Keep trying, Henry,"
she encouraged him.
"You are getting better!"

Soon it was the day of the
Summer Festival Dance.

Angelina and Henry
did not dance perfectly…
but they were close
enough!

Best of all,
they had lots of
fun dancing together!

Angelina and Henry
took a big bow,
and everyone cheered!